1812
Caroline's
BATTLE

BY KATHLEEN ERNST

ILLUSTRATIONS ROBERT PAPP

VIGNETTES LISA PAPP

★ American Girl®

THE AMERICAN GIRLS

1764 KAYA, an adventurous Nez Perce girl whose deep love for horses and respect for nature nourish her spirit

1774 FELICITY, a spunky, spritely colonial girl, full of energy and independence

1812 CAROLINE, a daring, self-reliant girl who learns to steer a steady course amid the challenges of war

1824 JOSEFINA, a Hispanic girl whose heart and hopes are as big as the New Mexico sky

1853 CÉCILE AND MARIE-GRACE, two girls whose friendship helps them—and New Orleans—survive terrible times

1854 KIRSTEN, a pioneer girl of strength and spirit who settles on the frontier

1864  ADDY, a courageous girl determined to be free in the midst of the Civil War

1904  SAMANTHA, a bright Victorian beauty, an orphan raised by her wealthy grandmother

1914  REBECCA, a lively girl with dramatic flair growing up in New York City

1934  KIT, a clever, resourceful girl facing the Great Depression with spirit and determination

1944  MOLLY, who schemes and dreams on the home front during World War Two

1974  JULIE, a fun-loving girl from San Francisco who faces big changes—and creates a few of her own

Published by American Girl Publishing
Copyright © 2012 by American Girl

Questions or comments? Call 1-800-845-0005, visit **americangirl.com**,
or write to Customer Service, American Girl, 8400 Fairway Place,
Middleton, WI 53562-0497.

Printed in China
12 13 14 15 16 17 LEO 10 9 8 7 6 5 4 3 2 1

Deep appreciation to Constance Barone, Director, Sackets Harbor Battlefield
State Historic Site; Dianne Graves, historian; James Spurr, historian and First Officer,
Friends Good Will, Michigan Maritime Museum; and Stephen Wallace,
former Interpretive Programs Assistant, Sackets Harbor Battlefield State Historic Site.
Sincere thanks also to the National Museum of American History, Smithsonian Institution.

PICTURE CREDITS

The following individuals and organizations have generously given permission to reprint
images contained in "Looking Back": p. 75—courtesy of the Smithsonian's National Museum of
American History; pp. 76–77—courtesy of Christopher G. Bova (Sackets Harbor); *British Attack
on Sackets Harbor on Lake Ontario, 1812,* detail, Library and Archives Canada, accession number
C-40598 (British warships); courtesy of Justin King (militiaman); pp. 78–79—courtesy of the
Beverley Robinson Collection, U.S. Naval Academy Museum, detail (*General Pike*); The White
House Historical Association (White House Collection), detail (Dolley Madison); North Wind
Picture Archives (Washington, D.C., burning); pp. 80–81—courtesy of Pickersgill Retirement
Community (Mary Pickersgill); courtesy of the Smithsonian's National Museum of American
History (museum display of flag); I.N. Phelps Stokes Collection, Miriam and Ira D. Wallach
Division of Art, Prints and Photographs, The New York Public Library, Astor, Lenox and Tilden
Foundations (bombardment over Fort McHenry); North Wind Picture Archives (Francis Scott
Key); courtesy of the Maryland Historical Society (sheet music); p. 82—© Image Source/Corbis.

Cataloging-in-Publication Data available from the Library of Congress

FOR CONSTANCE BARONE,
DIANNE GRAVES, JAMES SPURR,
AND STEPHEN WALLACE;
AND FOR EVERYONE WHO HAS
WORKED TO PRESERVE AND INTERPRET
SACKETS HARBOR'S RICH HERITAGE,
WITH TIIANKS

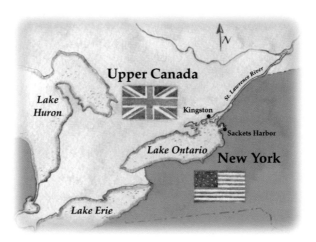

Caroline Abbott is growing up in Sackets Harbor, New York, right on the shore of Lake Ontario. Just across the lake is the British colony of *Upper Canada*.

In 1812, the nation of Canada didn't exist yet. Instead, the lands north of the Great Lakes were still a collection of British colonies. Today, Upper Canada is the Canadian province of Ontario.

In Caroline's time, there was a colony called *Lower Canada*, too. It stretched from Upper Canada eastward to the Atlantic Ocean. Today, it's the province of Quebec.

TABLE OF CONTENTS

CAROLINE'S FAMILY AND FRIENDS

CAROLINE'S FAMILY

PAPA
*Caroline's father, a
fine shipbuilder who
owns Abbott's Shipyard*

MAMA
*Caroline's mother, a firm
but understanding woman*

CAROLINE
*A daring girl who wants
to be captain of her
own ship one day*

GRANDMOTHER
*Mama's widowed mother,
who makes her home with
the Abbott family*

RHONDA HATHAWAY
*A twelve-year-old girl from the
big city of Albany who boards
at the Abbotts' house*

MRS. SHAW
*A neighbor who
sometimes finds fault
with Caroline*

MR. TATE
*The chief carpenter at
Abbott's and a good friend
of Caroline's family*

HOSEA BARTON
*A skilled sailmaker at
Abbott's Shipyard*

CHAPTER
ONE

—

SIGNAL GUNS!

Caroline Abbott tiptoed out of her house and closed the door behind her as silently as she could. It was hard to be quiet when she wanted to shout her good news from the rooftop! She hurried to the front gate and looked up and down the lane, hoping to see someone she knew passing by. Since America had gone to war with Great Britain, soldiers and sailors had flooded into the little village of Sackets Harbor, New York, and the lane was often bustling. Now, though, not a soul was in sight.

It's a fine May day, Caroline thought, *and I have no one to celebrate with!* Just when she was afraid she might burst, she spotted her neighbor coming outside

1

with a market basket over her arm. Caroline slipped out the gate and raced after the plump woman. "Mrs. Shaw!" she called. *"Mrs. Shaw!"*

Mrs. Shaw turned and waited for Caroline to join her. "Gracious, Caroline," Mrs. Shaw said sternly. "It isn't seemly for young ladies to race about—"

"Papa is home!" Caroline cried. She was ready to take her neighbor's arm and dance a jig! The British had captured Caroline's papa a year earlier and taken him to a fort in Upper Canada, across Lake Ontario. For many long months, Caroline and Mama hadn't heard a word from him.

Mrs. Shaw stared at her with wide eyes. "Heaven be praised," she whispered. "Did the British release him after all this time?"

"No, he escaped!" Caroline bounced on her toes. "He got away last autumn, but he broke his leg in the wilderness and couldn't travel all winter. He's been making his way here ever since spring came. I found him at his old fish camp! And I helped him walk home last night."

Mrs. Shaw gave Caroline a quick hug. "Is he well?"

"He hasn't had enough to eat," Caroline told

her. "And he needs to rest. He's sleeping now." Grandmother had sent Caroline outside to make sure that Papa could *continue* sleeping, actually, but Caroline didn't think Mrs. Shaw needed to know that.

Mrs. Shaw pulled out a handkerchief and wiped tears from her eyes. "I had given up hope," she admitted.

"*I* never did," Caroline said stoutly. It had been terribly hard to wait and wonder for so many months, but she had never lost hope.

"Well," Mrs. Shaw said, "you tell your father that I will bake a pie to welcome him home."

Caroline grinned. "I'll tell him," she promised.

Once Mrs. Shaw was on her way, Caroline tried to use up some of her bubbling energy by hoeing weeds in the garden. She and Grandmother had planted seeds earlier in the spring, and now tidy rows of tiny green seedlings marched across the soil. *Papa will eat some of those carrots and those peas!* Caroline thought happily. It felt like a miracle to have him home.

Hours seemed to pass before the kitchen door

3

opened and Mama stepped outside. Caroline dropped the hoe and darted over to join her. "Is Papa awake?" she asked.

Mama smiled. "He is. After a good meal and a hot bath last night, he slept soundly. He's already looking much better. He's coming downstairs for breakfast."

Caroline bounced on her toes again. "May I sit with him?"

"Garden chores can wait," Mama agreed. She smiled and kissed the top of Caroline's head. "Let's go inside."

Caroline, Mama, Grandmother, and Papa lingered at the kitchen table as he ate breakfast. Caroline was grateful that Mrs. Hathaway and her daughters, who boarded in the Abbotts' home, had kindly gone out to visit friends. "Your family needs a bit of privacy," Mrs. Hathaway had said.

Caroline sat on the bench next to Papa. *He's home,* she thought over and over. *Papa is home!*

"It does me more good than I can say to find my family well," Papa said. He finished a second biscuit.

"But—I've been afraid to ask—what has happened to the shipyard?"

"Abbott's Shipyard is doing a brisk business," Mama told him.

"It is?" Papa blinked, as if that was far better news than he'd expected. "I feared that once the war began, no one would order any new ships. I imagined I would find the shipyard closed and silent, and all the workers gone."

Grandmother chuckled. "You have a pleasant surprise waiting!"

"You'll be proud of the men when you see everything they've done," Caroline promised him.

Papa smiled at her and stroked her hair. "No doubt you're right, Caroline," he said. "I am eager to inspect the yard." He folded his napkin and put it aside. "We'll go at once."

Mama looked concerned. "Perhaps that should wait. Don't you want a few more days of rest?"

"No indeed," Papa said. "I've spent almost a year wondering how my business has been faring. And I already feel like a new man."

"I'll come too!" Caroline exclaimed.

Once Caroline and Mama had fetched their

shawls, the family set out, with Caroline on one arm and Mama on the other. *Papa does look like a new man,* Caroline thought, remembering how ragged he had looked when she'd found him at the fish camp. He still limped, and she realized sadly that he probably always would. But he had shaved, and Mama had cut his hair. His clothes looked big on his thin frame, but they were clean and free of holes.

"I hardly recognize our little village," Papa said, taking in the merchants' tents and hastily built taverns that had sprouted to serve all the soldiers, sailors, and shipbuilders who had arrived during his absence. Then the harbor came into view. Papa stopped walking and stared in astonishment.

Caroline tried to see the scene through Papa's eyes. Many things had changed while he was away. Each end of the harbor was now protected by a small log fort, with American flags proudly flying. She pointed to a narrow spit of land that stretched into the harbor. "We call that Navy Point now. See all those wooden buildings? Those are for military men and their supplies."

"So many soldiers and sailors are here now!" Papa marveled.

"Hundreds and hundreds," Caroline told him. "But a lot of them—like Lieutenant Hathaway—are away right now. They sailed off to Upper Canada more than a month ago to capture some forts." She tried to hide a shiver. She didn't like having so many sailors and soldiers gone. What if the British attacked?

Papa didn't seem to notice her unease. "And it seems that Abbott's is no longer the only shipyard in Sackets Harbor," he said. He stared at a new shipyard next to his own. It was much bigger than Abbott's and bustling with activity.

"The navy has established its own yard," Mama told him. "There are hundreds of shipwrights and carpenters in the village now."

Papa stared with admiration at a huge ship under construction in the navy yard. Caroline told him, "That frigate will be the mightiest ship ever to sail the Great Lakes! It's going to have twenty-eight cannons."

"Well, that should give the British trouble!" Papa said, rubbing his jaw.

"*Our* shipyard is giving the British trouble, too," Caroline told him proudly. "We're not making merchant sloops and schooners anymore. We're building gunboats for the navy."

Papa shook his head, as if trying to take in all the changes. "This is a much better homecoming than I could have imagined," he said.

Caroline slipped her arm through his. "Let's go see the men," she said. "They'll have a lot to show you."

The workmen at Abbott's were overjoyed to see Papa. Caroline laughed as they whooped and cheered and tossed their hats into the air. *How joyful it must be for Papa,* she thought, *to find his workers still here!*

Mr. Tate, the chief carpenter, pumped Papa's hand. "I always knew you'd come home, sir," he declared. "Indeed I did." His eyes sparkled with unshed tears.

For a moment Papa seemed unable to find words. He clenched Mr. Tate's hand. Caroline could see that her father was overwhelmed with emotion.

Finally Papa cleared his throat. "I'm very glad to be here," he said in a husky voice. "Now, I'd like to inspect the yard."

Mr. Tate showed him the gunboat the men were building. He explained everything they had learned as they switched from making trading ships to constructing heavy military boats. Caroline saw the workers listening carefully, as if hoping that Papa would approve of everything that had been done in his absence.

When the tour was complete, Papa declared, "I am more proud of you all than I can say. I spent months fearing that Abbott's Shipyard was no more. Instead, you've been helping to defend our country from our enemy!"

The men grinned and elbowed each other. Caroline was proud of them, too. She *knew* how hard they'd worked. She'd watched them.

Then Papa went to the office, and Mama showed him how she'd kept the books. "You managed all this?" Papa asked.

"Mama took charge right away," Caroline told him. "She's handled the contracts and made sure the men had the supplies they needed."

Papa looked startled. "I see," he said.

"I had a lot of help," Mama explained. "Mr. Tate watched over the workers, and Caroline helped me watch over the business accounts."

"Caroline?" Papa sounded taken aback, and he looked at her with an expression she didn't recognize. "My little girl, helping with the accounts?"

"I just tried to be helpful," Caroline said quickly. "I made copies of letters that Mama needed to send and checked the sums in the ledgers." She knew that Mama had given her those tasks largely so that Caroline could practice her penmanship and arithmetic. Even so, she'd taken pride in the work. She watched Papa, anxious to know that he was proud of her and of Mama, too.

"I see that I have much to learn," Papa said quietly. He didn't look at Caroline but instead settled on the high stool in front of his desk. He opened a ledger and began looking through the records.

"Caroline, perhaps you and I should take a stroll down the dock," Mama said. "It's such a fine day."

Caroline followed Mama outside. "Is something wrong?" she asked as she and Mama walked away from the office. "Is Papa displeased?"

10

"Not at all," Mama assured her. "You and I must try to remember that for all these months, Papa feared that his business would fail without him. He didn't expect to find Abbott's Shipyard busier than ever."

Caroline was still confused. "But... that's *good* news. I thought he would be happy!"

"He will be," Mama said. "But we must give Papa time to learn about all the changes that have taken place while he was away. Can you be patient with him?"

"Of course," Caroline said firmly. She would do anything she could to help Papa.

The next morning, Caroline came downstairs at dawn and found Grandmother and Mrs. Hathaway making breakfast. The bacon sizzling over the fire smelled so good that Caroline's stomach growled.

"Please set the dining-room table," Grandmother told Caroline. "Now that your father is home, we've too many people to fit here in the kitchen."

Once everyone had gathered around the table, Caroline introduced the boarders. "Papa, this is

Mrs. Hathaway and Rhonda and Amelia." She beamed. For many months, the Hathaways had heard stories about Papa. Now they could meet him in person!

Little Amelia was very quiet, sucking her thumb and watching him closely. Rhonda seemed unusually shy as well. "A pleasure to meet you, sir," she said. After a quick nod, she looked down at her plate.

Caroline nudged Rhonda under the table with her knee. Usually that would make Rhonda giggle and nudge back even harder. Today, though, Rhonda didn't respond. Caroline was puzzled by her friend's mood.

Suddenly, Caroline realized why Rhonda was being quiet. *Everything's turned upside down,* Caroline thought. *I used to envy Rhonda because **her** father was nearby.* Now Papa was home, and Rhonda's father was off on a dangerous expedition. Caroline leaned close enough to whisper in her friend's ear, "Your father will be back soon, and—"

Boom! Boom! Caroline looked up sharply and clapped her hands over her ears as cannon fire shuddered through the air. The windowpanes rattled, and it felt as if her bones rattled too.

Papa dropped his fork with a clatter. Mama's face went white.

Not today, Caroline thought. She felt numb with disbelief. "Those shots came from the big guns at the forts," she said. "Sackets Harbor must be under attack!"

Papa's hands curled into fists. His face settled into hard lines.

Caroline jumped to her feet. She ran from the dining room and out the front door. She had to find out what was happening! Her family and the Hathaways joined her just as a young man on horseback clattered toward them.

Papa stepped to the gate and waved a hand. "*Sir!*" he barked in his ship-captain voice. "What's happening?"

The young man pulled his horse to a stop. "A British fleet has been sighted about seven miles from here," he told them, breathing hard. "I'm with the militia, on my way to spread the word."

"How large is the fleet?" Papa demanded.

"There are probably a thousand enemy men out there," the militiaman said. "And when they land, they'll have their ships' cannons to protect them."

*The young man pulled his horse to a stop. "A British fleet has been sighted,"
he told them. "There are probably a thousand enemy men out there."*

A thousand men? Caroline felt anger boil up inside. "Hateful British! I wish they would just leave us *alone*!"

Papa squinted the way he sometimes did when he was sailing a ship and making a judgment about the weather. "There's no wind," he said.

"Aye," the soldier agreed. "Those ships can't move with no wind in their sails. That gives us some time to call in the militia. Now, I must be off." He kicked his horse to a gallop, and everyone watched him pound away.

Mama murmured, "Thank heavens the British weren't able to surprise our men."

"But the wind could start blowing again any moment!" Caroline said.

"It could." Papa nodded. "The wind could pick up again an hour from now, or a day from now. We must use whatever time we have to prepare for the attack."

Grandmother leaned on her cane with both hands. "We've known they would come sooner or later," she said. "They're after that big new frigate the navy's building, I'd wager."

"But most of our soldiers and sailors are

away!" Rhonda cried. "There's hardly anyone left to defend us!"

"Those alarm guns were meant to call out the militia," Grandmother reminded Rhonda. "And riders like that young man will be on their way to distant farms where the men might not hear the guns. Our militiamen will be ready to meet the British."

Caroline understood why Rhonda sounded frightened. She was frightened, too. She had seen the militia drilling in town, practicing for a battle. The farmers and workmen were not nearly as well trained as the army and navy men.

Another deafening *boom-boom* sounded as the signal guns repeated their message. "Come, girls," Mrs. Hathaway said quietly to Rhonda and Amelia. She shepherded her daughters back inside.

Caroline glanced at Papa. He looked grim. *What a terrible homecoming,* Caroline thought.

For a long moment, no one spoke. Then Papa turned to his wife. "I must go."

"What?" Mama gasped.

"Go where?" Caroline asked at the same time.

Papa said, "To volunteer with the militia."

"Papa, no!" Caroline cried. How could he leave? She'd just gotten him back!

Mama clutched his arm. "You're not yet well."

"I'm well enough," Papa said. "I can handle a musket. Sackets Harbor needs every man to fight."

Caroline grabbed Papa's free hand. *If I never let go*, she thought, *maybe Papa won't leave.* She watched her parents anxiously.

"I don't *want* to go," Papa said to them. "But I think you understand why I must."

"But you just got home," Caroline protested. "It's not *fair*!"

"It isn't fair," Papa agreed. He squeezed her hand. "But life is not always fair, especially in times of war."

Mama still looked worried, but she nodded. "Very well," she said. "You join the militia and defend the village. But the gunboat and our shipbuilding supplies must be protected as well. I'll keep watch at the shipyard."

Papa shook his head. "You will not! Mr. Tate and the men will defend the shipyard. You and your mother and Caroline must take shelter in the root cellar." He put one arm around Caroline's shoulders. She burrowed closer, wishing she could stay beside him forever.

Papa added, "I don't want to join the militia without knowing that all of you are safely away from the fighting."

He sounded so worried that Caroline knew she had to help ease his mind. "We'll stay safe," she promised, but it was hard to squeeze the words around the lump in her throat.

BAD NEWS
AT THE SHIPYARD

When the Abbotts went back inside, they found the Hathaways in the hallway with packed carpetbags. "My husband gave me firm instructions about what to do during an attack," Mrs. Hathaway explained. "I must take the girls inland, away from the fighting. We'll find shelter with a farm family we met as we traveled here last fall." She looked at Mama. "We could all go together."

"Thank you for the offer," Mama told her. "But we have property to protect. I will not leave Sackets Harbor."

Caroline knew that many women and children would be leaving the village, hoping to get far away before the fighting started. She was frightened too, but like Mama, she didn't want to leave her home.

"We'll be safe enough in the root cellar," Grandmother added briskly. "Once the Americans drive the British away, we'll be waiting for your return."

"Very well." Mrs. Hathaway nodded. "Be safe, my dear friends. God willing, we'll all be together again."

Rhonda and Caroline hugged each other. "Come back soon," Caroline whispered.

"As soon as we can," Rhonda whispered back. Mrs. Hathaway led her daughters away.

Caroline stayed close to Papa as he fetched his old musket, cleaned it well, and packed ammunition in a pouch. She could hardly believe that Papa was leaving again.

Once his preparations were made, Papa led his family outside. Scary pictures formed in Caroline's mind. What if Papa were wounded in battle? What if he got *killed*? She threw her arms around him. "I wish you weren't going!"

"There, now." Papa stroked her hair. "A man

must protect his home and family. I need to do my part."

Caroline struggled to keep from crying. *Don't make this harder on Papa than it is already,* she told herself sternly, but she couldn't seem to loosen her grip around Papa's waist.

He gently pulled away from her. "You be careful, daughter," he said. "Help your mama and grandmother as best you can."

"I—I will," Caroline promised. She blinked hard as her eyes filled with tears.

"Once we've sent the British back to Upper Canada, I will lay down my musket and get back to work as a shipbuilder," he added. "Remembering busy days at Abbott's Shipyard helped me survive while I was a prisoner. Imagining us all working there together will help me survive this day, too."

Papa kissed Mama, Grandmother, and Caroline good-bye. Then he limped away. The lane was busy with traffic now—militiamen rushing to their posts, riders carrying news, women and children hurrying away from the village with bundles and sacks. As Caroline watched, Papa was quickly swallowed by the crowd.

Mama and Grandmother turned to go inside. Caroline paused, sniffing the air to see if a breeze had come up yet. The morning was heavy and still, with low clouds that threatened rain. Every leaf on every tree hung motionless.

The British must still be offshore, impatiently waiting for a wind to fill their sails, thought Caroline. *All* ***we*** *can do now is wait, too.* There was no way to predict when a wind might blow the British fleet toward Sackets Harbor.

When Caroline followed Mama and Grand-mother back inside, the house seemed terribly silent. *What should I do now?* Caroline wondered, twisting her hands together. She wished there were something she could do to help Papa and the other American fighters. It was so hard to simply wait for the attack to begin!

Grandmother gave Caroline a meaningful look. "At such times, it's best to stay busy. I've already started heating the bake oven. I'll make a double batch of bread today. There may be hungry soldiers needing food before too long."

Mama had been standing very still, her

head tipped thoughtfully to one side. Suddenly she reached for her bonnet and cape, which were hanging on a stand by the front door.

"Mama?" Caroline asked. "Where are you going?"

"I am going to the shipyard," Mama said. Grandmother chuckled and nodded, as if she'd been expecting this.

Caroline, though, had not. "But Papa said—"

"Papa said the workers would guard the gunboat and building supplies," Mama said. "And they will. But I've been thinking. Papa hasn't seen all the important records that are stored in the office now. Designs for gunboats, instructions from the navy— the British would probably value those things even more than the gunboat itself."

Caroline pressed a hand over her mouth. She hadn't thought about that! But Mama was right— if the British got their hands on the plans created by America's finest shipbuilders, they could use the new ideas and designs in their *own* ships.

"I am determined to remove as many documents as I can before the wind picks up," Mama added. "We'll hide them here at home."

Caroline's spirits rose. Surely Papa would understand why Mama was acting against his instructions. Besides, she welcomed the idea of *doing* something to help beat the British. "May I come with you? *Please? I want to help!"*

"Yes indeed," Mama said. "Go fetch the big gathering baskets from the kitchen."

As Caroline raced to do Mama's bidding, she sent a silent message to the British men on their ships. *We will not give up easily,* she warned them. The Abbotts, each in their own way, were ready to fight.

In a few minutes Caroline and Mama set off, each carrying two empty baskets. A light rain drizzled from the clouds, but the air remained still. Caroline pressed close to Mama, for Main Street was mobbed. Men on horseback trotted past. Army men drove supply wagons through town, trying to remove anything the British might steal. Near the harbor, traffic had halted altogether because a family's cart had broken its axle.

"This way!" Mama called, leading Caroline

through the noisy commotion. Caroline clutched her baskets tightly so that they wouldn't get jostled from her hands.

When they reached Abbott's, Caroline saw the workers standing guard around the shipyard, armed with broadaxes and mallets. It hurt Caroline's heart to see shipbuilding tools used as weapons, but she was more proud of the men than ever.

Mr. Tate hurried to greet them, carrying his ancient musket. "I didn't expect to see you, ma'am!" he exclaimed. "And Miss Caroline as well! Where is Mr. Abbott?"

"Papa left to join the militia," Caroline told him.

Mr. Tate shook his head. "And him just newly arrived home? *Blast* the British."

"I see that you and the men are set to defend the yard," Mama said. "Well done. Caroline and I are going to haul off whatever records and plans we can carry."

Mr. Tate gave a quick, satisfied nod. "I'll leave you to it," he said.

Caroline and Mama hurried into the office. "Roll up those plans," Mama said, pointing to the large sketches Mr. Tate had made to guide the carpenters building the gunboat outside. "I'll gather the ledgers."

Caroline did as she was told, quickly rolling up the large pieces of parchment and tying them with string. Then she filled her baskets with account books and the letters that Mama had exchanged with the U.S. Navy officers who had hired Abbott's to build gunboats.

With their loaded baskets, Caroline and Mama struggled more than ever to make their way through the crowded streets. By the time they reached home, Caroline's arms ached. Her toes ached, too, for several people had stepped on them as she'd wormed her way through the crowds.

Grandmother met them at the kitchen door. "Empty the baskets, and leave everything to me," she said. "I know a thing or two about hiding valuables from British soldiers."

Caroline didn't doubt that! Grandmother had lived through the American Revolution thirty years earlier, doing everything she could to help defeat the British. "We're going back for another load," Caroline told her. She piled the contents of her baskets on the kitchen table.

Grandmother gave Mama a sideways glance. There was a question in her eyes.

"There is still no wind," Mama told her. Caroline nodded. She and Mama were paying attention to the weather. If even a breath of wind came up, they'd notice right away.

"Get on with it, then." Grandmother made a shooing gesture.

Caroline and Mama made their way back to the harbor. Suddenly Caroline heard a faint rattle of musket fire in the distance.

"I don't like the sound of that," Mama said grimly.

"How could there be fighting already?" Caroline burst out. "I thought the British were stuck offshore!" Were British soldiers already marching toward Sackets Harbor? Was Papa already in the midst of fighting, already in danger? Caroline shivered. They had no way of knowing what was happening even a few miles away.

"Perhaps the British got tired of waiting and rowed some men ashore," Mama said. "If so, they can't have landed many soldiers. Still, we must hurry." She grabbed Caroline's arm as they elbowed their way toward the yard. Caroline was glad to feel Mama's firm grasp.

When they reached Abbott's again, Caroline expected to see the workers still standing guard. Instead, the men had gathered in a clump near the entrance. Mr. Tate seemed to be arguing with a man in an American military uniform. *Oh no*, Caroline thought. *What now?*

Mama hurried to join the conversation. Caroline wanted to hear too, and followed on Mama's heels. Caroline could tell by the fancy braid on the soldier's coat that he was an officer. He had gray hair, and there were dark circles beneath his eyes.

"Gentlemen!" Mama said in a tone that stopped the discussion. She introduced herself to the officer. "I'm in charge of the shipyard when my husband is away," she told him. "What's happening?" She gestured toward the far-off sound of muskets.

"A few dozen British men and some of their Indian allies rowed ashore several miles west of here," the officer said. "As soon as the wind picks up, though, the British fleet will surely head for Sackets Harbor and try to land a huge force near the village."

Caroline swallowed hard as she imagined hundreds of British soldiers and sailors fighting their way into her village. The drizzle suddenly seemed very cold.

Mama pinched her lips together for a moment. Then she said, "I understand, sir. But what is your business here?"

The officer waved his hand toward the shipyard. "I need these men to help defend Navy Point."

Caroline caught her breath. She saw the men exchanging worried glances and heard them muttering in protest. "We're needed here, to guard the gunboat!" one of the carpenters shouted.

"With so many of the American troops away, our position is desperate," the officer snapped. "We need every man to fight."

"But—but sir," Caroline stammered, "who will defend our shipyard?"

"Let us pray the British won't reach the ship-yards," he said. "Now, all of you men—line up. Bring whatever weapons you have."

Mr. Tate looked at Mama. "Ma'am?"

"Do as he says," Mama told him quietly. She turned to the workers. "Please take care of yourselves."

With dismay, Caroline watched the shipbuilders form a ragged line. These were the men who'd kept Abbott's Shipyard going, who had been kind and patient with her, who had lifted her spirits during the difficult last year. Now they were ready to do what was necessary to defend Sackets Harbor. She knew that the men would do Abbott's proud, just as they always had, but she hated to see them go.

Hosea Barton, the sailmaker, paused beside her. "Don't worry, Miss Caroline. We'll be back. We've got a gunboat to finish."

Mr. Tate was the last to leave. "Mrs. Abbott, I'm sorry," he said. "What will you do?"

"I'll do whatever I must," Mama said. Her voice was calm, but Caroline saw that she'd clenched folds of her cape into her fists. "Thank you, sir, for everything."

Mr. Tate nodded, tugged his hat down over his eyes, and propped his musket over one shoulder. Then he turned and joined the other men as they tramped away.

Caroline and Mama stood still and watched them go. The day's noise and commotion suddenly seemed distant. *I've never seen the shipyard empty before*, Caroline thought. She'd visited Abbott's in the morning, at midday, in the evening ... and always, *always*, at least some of the men were there.

Now Abbott's was quiet. The yard was deserted. A battle was brewing, and Caroline and Mama were alone.

CHAPTER THREE

TERRIBLE ORDERS

Caroline and Mama watched the workers until they disappeared from view. The musket fire in the distance had stopped. The new silence seemed terrible and threatening.

Finally Mama turned toward the office. "We must make haste," she said. "I want you to take one last batch of records home."

Caroline's mouth went dry as she realized that Mama was sending her back alone. She remembered what Mama had told Mr. Tate: *I'll do whatever I must.*

Mama put her hands on Caroline's shoulders and looked her straight in the eye. "I'm staying here at the yard."

"But, Mama," Caroline protested, "Papa told us to take shelter in the root cellar, where we'll be safe!"

"Yes, he did," Mama said soberly. "But Papa didn't know that all the workers would be pulled away to help defend the village. The situation has changed, Caroline. Now I must do what I think is best. I trust that Papa will understand."

Caroline hated leaving Mama all alone at the shipyard. Still, she knew that Mama needed help, not arguments, so she held her protests inside. "Yes, Mama," she said reluctantly. "I'll go."

In the office, Caroline helped pack two baskets with the last ledger and letters. "Once you're back at the house," Mama said, "take Grandmother into the root cellar. A wind might spring up at any minute and fill those British sails!" After kissing Caroline on the forehead, Mama gave her a little push toward the door.

Caroline hurried back through Sackets Harbor. There were no women or children in sight. Caroline knew that they were either safely away or sheltering inside their own cellars by now. It felt strange, and a little spooky, to be alone among soldiers and militiamen who were thinking only of battle. When

Caroline reached her house, she scurried inside and closed the door behind her with a *whoosh* of relief.

When she told Grandmother about Mama's decision, the old woman did not look surprised. "I wouldn't expect your mother to do anything less," Grandmother said. "She's a brave woman."

Caroline nodded. Grandmother and Mama were *both* brave women. Caroline hoped that she might one day prove herself to be as smart and courageous as they were.

Grandmother rubbed her chin, looking about the kitchen. "There's no telling how long she'll have to stay at the shipyard," she murmured. "Tell me, Caroline, is there any wind yet?"

"No, ma'am," Caroline said. "The lake is as still as a bowl of milk."

"Good. I want to send some food and a blanket down to your mother. Will you make one more trip to the yard?" Grandmother looked at her intently.

Caroline blinked in surprise. Mama had instructed her to stay safely at home until the battle was over! *But Grandmother is right,* Caroline thought. There was no way to know how long Mama might be alone at the shipyard. And Mama had said that sometimes, in difficult situations, people need to make their own choices.

Caroline squared her shoulders. "Yes, I will," she told Grandmother. "I'll run like a deer."

Grandmother smiled. "That's the spirit," she said. "I've got beans and bacon warm over the fire. Fetch a plate and have a good meal yourself, and I'll prepare some supplies for your mother."

Caroline hadn't thought she was hungry, but with one bite of the sweet and salty baked beans, she changed her mind. By the time she'd gobbled her helping and eaten a piece of warm bread dripping with butter, Grandmother had joined her again.

"Here's the basket," Grandmother began. "I want you to see what I've packed."

Caroline scrambled to her feet, wiping her mouth with a napkin. "I'm sure Mama will be pleased with whatever you send, Grandmother."

"I want you to see what I've packed," Grandmother repeated. Her voice was unusually slow and forceful.

Caroline went still. Something was on Grandmother's mind.

"I've put in two loaves of bread, the last of the

dried apples, and some smoked fish." Grandmother gestured at each of the items. Then she lifted the corner of a cloth she'd put under the food. "And something else your mama might need."

Caroline's eyes went wide as she saw the silver glint of metal. Grandmother had hidden a pistol under the cloth. Nestled beside it was a little sack that no doubt held ammunition.

Grandmother tucked the cloth back in place. "You must deliver this to your mother's hands."

"Yes, ma'am," Caroline whispered. The sight of the gun made her feel shivery inside. Many years ago, Papa had ordered Caroline not to touch either of his guns, and she never had. *But I must carry this pistol to Mama*, she thought. The only way Mama would have a gun to help defend Abbott's was if Caroline took it to her.

"One more thing." Grandmother cupped Caroline's face in her hands. "I'm an old woman. I've lived through more than one battle. As soon as trouble starts, I will settle myself in the root cellar, safe from enemy gunfire. I'm not afraid to be alone. Do you understand?"

Caroline's eyes went wide as she saw the silver glint of metal.

Caroline swallowed hard. Grandmother's eyes held everything that she didn't say: *Make your own decision about coming home, my girl. If you feel that you should stay with your mama, do not worry about me.* Now Caroline understood why Grandmother had insisted that she eat a hearty meal before heading back to the shipyard.

It took Caroline a moment to find her voice. Finally she took a deep breath. "Yes, Grandmother," she said. "I understand."

"Good girl." Grandmother patted Caroline's cheek.

Caroline put on her cloak, picked up the blanket roll that Grandmother had prepared, and hooked the basket handle over one arm. "I'll do my best," she promised.

"I know you will." Grandmother nodded. "Off you go."

Caroline hurried back to Abbott's Shipyard. The office was on the ground floor of the main shipyard building, close to the street. When Caroline looked inside, she found the room empty. Next she checked the workshops behind the office. They were empty too. Perhaps Mama was up in the sail loft. The big

room where Hosea stitched
huge sails was on the second
story of the building. From
the window there, Mama
would be able to see the half-
built gunboat in the yard below. She'd also be able
to see the harbor.

Mama came running when she heard footsteps
on the stairs. "Caroline!" she cried. "I expected you
to stay home!"

"I know," Caroline said quickly. "But Grandmother asked me to bring you some supplies." She
put the basket on a bench and showed Mama what
had been packed inside.

"That was thoughtful," Mama said as she saw
the food. "And—ah." Caroline had lifted the cloth,
revealing the pistol. Mama pulled the gun free,
loaded it, and slipped it into a pocket.

Caroline looked around the empty loft. Through
the window, she could see the empty yard. *I need
to stay here*, Caroline thought. She hoped Mama
wouldn't order her to go back home. She felt her
hands tremble and clutched them together behind
her back so that Mama wouldn't see.

Then Caroline lifted her chin. "Grandmother told me she would be fine alone," she said firmly. "You need help more than she does. I'm going to stay here with you, Mama."

For a moment Caroline thought Mama was going to disagree. Caroline forced herself to hold her mother's gaze. *I can do it,* she told Mama silently. *I can be brave and help protect Abbott's Shipyard.*

Finally Mama nodded. "Very well, Caroline," she said. "Thank you. The yard is a lonely place with all the men gone. I'll be glad of your company."

Mama stayed up in the sail loft, where she could see the street and yard below and look out on the harbor. Caroline kept watch from the office doorway, wrapped in her cloak. Militiamen jogged past all afternoon, splashing through puddles in ones and twos and groups. They'd come from distant farms and villages to join the line of men defending Sackets Harbor. The sight of the men, hard-faced and ready to fight, made Caroline's stomach tumble. Sometimes she glanced up for reassurance at the

"Abbott's" sign that hung over the entrance to the yard. *Abbott's Shipyard is here to stay,* she thought stubbornly, *and so am I.*

Once, an army officer hurried by. "Any news?" Caroline called.

"Those British ships still can't move," he told her. "Their sails are hanging limp as laundry on the line."

Caroline *almost* wished the wind would pick up. It was so difficult to simply wait, wait, *wait!*

The sun was setting when a young man in navy uniform raced into Abbott's Shipyard, his hat pulled low against the light rain. "Halloo the yard!" he hollered. "Mrs. Abbott?" He leaned over, panting for breath.

Caroline quickly stepped from the doorway and introduced herself. "My mother is keeping watch upstairs," she told him.

Mama leaned out the window. "I'll be right down, Corporal Meyers!" she called. A few moments later, she hurried from the building and joined them. "What's the news?" she asked at once.

"You've probably heard that a small British force landed west of here this morning," Corporal Meyers said.

"What happened?" Caroline asked anxiously.

"The fighting went badly for us," he said. "Some of the Americans retreated. Others surrendered, blast their hides."

Caroline leaned against Mama.

"As soon as the weather changes, the British will surely attack Sackets Harbor," Corporal Meyers continued. "We're preparing bonfires in the navy shipyard."

"Preparing *bonfires*?" Caroline asked. "Why?"

Corporal Meyers jerked his head toward the huge warship that was under construction in the navy yard. "If the British fight their way through the line of Americans defending the harbor, we will burn the navy shipyard and destroy our new frigate. Whatever else happens, we must not let that ship fall into enemy hands!"

Caroline followed his gaze. The navy workers had framed up the ship and begun nailing planks in place. She knew the Americans needed that mighty ship to take control of Lake Ontario and help win the war.

"Ma'am, you must make the same plans," Corporal Meyers told Mama. "Prepare bonfires, and torches as well."

Caroline stared at him. His words were quite clear, and yet she had a hard time taking in his meaning. *He wants us to burn Abbott's if our soldiers can't stop the British,* she thought. She felt numb.

"I understand," Mama told Corporal Meyers. She reached for Caroline's hand and squeezed. "We'll prepare."

Caroline opened her mouth, but no words came out. She felt as if the world were suddenly spinning in circles and the only thing keeping her feet planted on the ground was Mama's grip.

"If all is lost, we'll set fire to the barracks and storehouses on Navy Point," the corporal told them. "You'll see the flames. That will be your signal."

Mama nodded. "Very well."

"May God protect us," Corporal Meyers said. For just a moment, he looked more like a frightened farmboy than a military man. Then he tipped his hat before running off again.

"Mama?" Caroline's voice shook. "Did you really mean...?" She couldn't finish the sentence.

"We must not let Abbott's fall into enemy hands!" Mama said fiercely. "The gunboat, all our tools and supplies—it's better to destroy them than let the

British take them and use them against us."

Caroline desperately wanted to pretend that none of this was happening. How could her mother even consider this dreadful thing? "Oh, Mama," she said, "we *can't* burn the shipyard!"

"I pray we won't have to," Mama replied. "But we must be prepared to do so if necessary."

In the twilight, Caroline looked around the yard. Papa had worked for years to build his business. And Mama and the Abbott's men had worked night and day to keep it going while they waited for Papa to come home. *How can we destroy it?* she asked herself. How would Papa feel if he returned and saw nothing but ashes?

"Mama..." Caroline's throat felt thick with panic. "Papa's heart will break if we burn the yard!"

For a long moment, Mama stared silently at the shipyard. "I know," she said finally. "But if we must, I think Papa will understand that we did what we had to do."

Caroline still wasn't sure. "Mama? How do you know when it's right to do what you're told, and when to decide for yourself?"

Mama looked down and held Caroline's gaze.

"It is sometimes very difficult," she admitted. "I try to use both my mind and my heart."

Caroline was silent. Her mind said that burning the shipyard if the Americans were defeated was the right thing to do. Her heart said that burning the shipyard would be horribly wrong.

"I wish Papa were here," Caroline whispered.

"I wish he were here, too," Mama said. "But he isn't, so we must simply do the best we can." She blew out a long breath before adding, "You chose to stay here with me, Caroline. Now you must stand tall, because I truly need your help."

For a moment Caroline wished she *had* stayed at home with Grandmother. If she had, she wouldn't have to face Corporal Meyers' terrible orders.

Seconds seemed to tick past in Caroline's mind, loud as a mantel clock. Finally she thought, *Mama is right.* She had chosen to stay. Now she had to be steady and face whatever had to be faced.

"I'll help you, Mama," Caroline said at last. Her voice still shook a little, and she struggled to firm it up. "Tell me what I need to do."

THE BATTLE

As twilight's shadows stretched across the shipyard, Caroline and Mama got busy gathering wood. "We'll start the bonfire," Mama said, "and keep it blazing so that we can light torches quickly if we need to burn the yard."

Caroline knew it wouldn't be hard to burn the shipyard to the ground. Almost everything—the workshops, the storage sheds, and the gunboat itself—was made of wood. Piles of logs and sawn boards sat about, too. Guarding against fire was an everyday habit for her family and the workers. Barrels full of water stood near the door to every workshop, with buckets ready to quickly douse any accidental blaze.

Now, though, she needed to think about *starting*

a fire. "There are piles of wood shavings in the carpentry shops," Caroline said. "Those will catch fire easily. Shall I gather some?"

Mama nodded. "That will do nicely."

Caroline ran to the nearest shop. The floor was littered with tiny curls of wood, left when the carpenters had carefully shaved pieces of wood to the exact shape they needed. Caroline quickly swept some shavings into a pile and filled a pail with the delicate bits.

Back outside, Caroline scanned the yard. The main building stood near the road. An open area, wide enough that the men could work with the huge trees they cut and dragged to the yard, stretched between the building and the half-built gunboat. Wooden support beams held the gunboat in place, pointed at the harbor so that it would be ready to slide into the water when it was finished. Small storage sheds squatted near the dock close by.

Where should they build the fire? The rain would make tending it difficult. Caroline decided on an open-air shelter where the carpenters sometimes worked, near the main building. The roof, held up by four tall posts, would help keep the firewood dry.

From that spot, it would be easy to set fire to the sheds and the main building. After that, she and Mama could quickly run across the yard and set the gunboat on fire.

Caroline dumped the wood shavings in a pile beneath the shelter. Then she ran back to the shop and fetched an armful of bigger pieces of wood— stray chunks the men had tossed into one corner. She carried them to the shelter. Mama dragged over some boards.

When Caroline and Mama had gathered a good supply of wood, they built the fire, arranging kindling around a pile of shavings. Mama lit the shavings. Caroline carefully blew on them until the flames grew tall enough to catch the kindling. Soon the fire was snapping and crackling, bright against the deepening shadows.

"Well done," Mama said.

Caroline sat back on her heels and looked toward the navy shipyard. She could see a bonfire burning there, too. Its flickering glow was comforting, in a way. It reminded her that at least a few navy men were standing guard nearby. Caroline just hoped that the bonfires would not have to be used for anything more than keeping them warm that night.

"What else?" she asked Mama.

"Let's gather more wood shavings and scatter them about the workshops, the office, and the sheds," Mama said. "If we do have to burn the yard, we'll want everything to catch fire quickly."

Caroline clenched her teeth as she walked through the familiar rooms, helping to prepare them for destruction. *This feels like a bad dream!* she thought. If only she could wake up and snuggle with her cat, Inkpot, and tell him all about the nightmare she'd had of burning Abbott's.

Finally, only the torches were left to prepare. Full darkness had settled over Sackets Harbor. Mama lit two lanterns and handed one to Caroline. "I'll find two stout sticks," Mama said. "Would you fetch some cloth, some twine, and the extra lamp oil?"

Caroline carried the lantern with great care as she walked through the sail loft to fetch cloth and went into the office to fetch twine and lamp oil. With wood shavings scattered about everywhere, she knew that if she stumbled and dropped the lantern, she might start a fire by accident.

She joined Mama at the bonfire. Mama handed

her a long, heavy pole. She held it still while Mama wrapped cloth around one end and tied it in place with the twine. Then they prepared the second torch.

"Now, let's step well away from the fire," Mama said. Caroline caught a sharp whiff of lamp oil as Mama soaked the cloth. Caroline knew that after being drenched with the oil, the torch would need only a spark to catch fire. Once the torches were prepared, Mama laid them on bare ground a safe distance from the blaze.

Caroline scanned the shipyard, trying to steady herself. *If I must help burn the yard, I'll start with the skiff shed,* she thought. She had sunk her family's skiff a few days earlier while saving an American supply ship, so the shed was empty.

With preparations complete, Caroline and Mama shared some of the food Grandmother had sent. Then Caroline helped Mama make a rough bed in the office. "One of us can sleep while one stands watch," Mama said.

"You can rest first, Mama," Caroline offered. She was tired, but she felt too jittery to sleep right away.

Mama nodded. "Very well. Be sure to tend the fire regularly. If you see or hear anything in the yard, come inside and wake me at once!"

Caroline crept out to the bonfire, found a log to sit on, and settled down to watch. The air was cold and damp. Raindrops dripped from the shelter roof. The shipyard was cloaked in darkness. She reminded herself that American soldiers and volunteers, including Papa, would do their best to keep the British away from Abbott's and the navy shipyard. But if they failed, and the British broke through... Caroline rubbed her eyes, trying to clear the picture of Abbott's in flames from her imagination.

A sudden rustle nearby made her jump. *That was likely just a mouse*, Caroline thought. Still, she added another chunk of wood to the fire. She welcomed its light.

Shivering, Caroline pulled her cloak tightly around her. Waiting all day for the British attack had been almost unbearable, but waiting at night was even worse. She had nothing to do but stare out at the dark yard, alone with her thoughts. Where was Papa right now? Was he trying to sleep on the cold ground, or perhaps keeping watch as she was? Did he have any notion that his precious shipyard might be destroyed by the time the battle ended?

Caroline tried to rub away the goose bumps on her arms. It was going to be a long night.

Caroline kept watch until she felt ready to sleep. Then she went inside, woke Mama, and curled up on the blanket.

She felt as if she'd barely drifted off to sleep when Mama touched her shoulder. "Your turn," Mama said.

Caroline yawned as she stumbled to her feet and headed back outside. The night had grown colder, and the damp air seeped through her cloak. Once she was perched on the log by the bonfire, she sat staring into the darkness beyond the shadows cast by the flames. *I must stay alert,* she reminded herself. If only her eyes didn't feel so sandy. If only she had something to do besides sit and think. Except for the crackling fire, everything seemed quiet—

Caroline jerked upright as a shadow moved across the yard, near the gunboat. She strained to see against the darkness. Yes! There it was again. Her heart suddenly seemed to beat much too fast.

She jumped to her feet and silently scurried back to the office. She eased the door open and slipped inside. "Mama, someone's out there!" she hissed.

Her mother scrambled to her feet. As she and Caroline peered out the window, a second shadowy figure darted through the yard. He was visible in the fire glow for a moment, then gone.

Mama stepped to the door and cracked it open again. Caroline saw the silhouette of the pistol in Mama's hand. "Who's there?" Mama demanded in a terrible voice.

There was no answer.

"I'm a good shot," Mama warned. Caroline held her breath. Would Mama have to use the pistol?

A man's voice came from the yard. "We mean no harm."

"Be on your way!" Mama ordered.

The same voice spoke. "We're just two soldiers looking for a dry spot to sleep—"

Mama raised her hand and fired at the sky. Caroline jumped.

"You won't find your rest here tonight," Mama

told the men. "Be on your way. Next time I won't aim for the clouds."

Through the window, Caroline saw two shadows dart back through the yard, heading toward the road. Mama waited for several more moments before closing the door again. "They've gone," she reported. She leaned against the closed door.

Caroline's heartbeat began to slow. "Why did you scare those men away?" she asked. "It's a cold, wet night, and if all they wanted was shelter..."

"If those men are American soldiers, they belong with their comrades," Mama said. "But what if they were thieves, or British spies? I'll have no strangers sneaking through our shipyard in the darkness."

Mama's right, Caroline thought. She took a deep breath and blew it out slowly. "It's a good thing Grandmother packed that pistol."

Mama reached out and squeezed Caroline's hand. "And a good thing you were willing to bring it."

Boom! Boom-boom!
Caroline jerked up from her blanket on the floor.

Mama had taken the last watch, and now dawn was just beginning to lighten the day.

Boom-boom-boom!

"Oh!" Caroline gasped. Cannons were firing steadily, close enough and loud enough to make her rib cage quiver. The British must have landed! She pulled on her shoes and raced outside.

The rain had stopped. Mama stood by the bonfire, arms crossed, listening. "Are we under attack?" Caroline cried. She lifted her face toward the sky. Wind shoved at her hair.

"The main British fleet must have landed—very close to town," Mama said.

Beneath the cannons' thunder, Caroline made out the rattle of muskets. The American men—*Papa!*—must be trying to fight off the British soldiers who'd landed.

"I'm going up to the sail loft," Mama said.

Caroline nodded. From the loft, it would be easier for Mama to see Navy Point, where—if needed—American men would send the signal to burn the shipyards.

Mama put her hands on Caroline's shoulders, as she had done the day before. "Keep the bonfire

burning. You may not be able to hear me call, so if
I wave my arms at you, that will be your sign to light
a torch and get to work."

"Yes, Mama," Caroline whispered. A shiver iced
down her backbone, as if a bit of snow had slipped
inside her collar.

"And I'll run down and destroy the gunboat,"
Mama said. "I saved some lamp oil to pour on the
boat so that it will burn quickly. You set fire to
the buildings."

Caroline took a deep breath. "I'll be ready."

"Remember, watch for my signal. God bless you,
child. Stay safe." Mama kissed Caroline's forehead.
Then she picked up her skirts and ran toward the
sail loft.

Caroline decided to stand near the street,
halfway between the main building and the gunboat.
From there she could easily see the sail-loft window
and could quickly grab a torch. She'd also be able to
hear news from anyone passing by. Once she was
in place, though, it was hard to stand still. Her skin
tingled. Her hands trembled. She felt sick to her
stomach.

This won't do, Caroline told herself sternly. It was

too early to give up hope. Perhaps the American fighters would drive the enemy back before they came anywhere near the shipyard. Perhaps Mama would never have to give the signal to burn Abbott's. Caroline sent a silent message to Papa and the rest of the American men. *Hold strong. Don't let the British break through.*

Caroline left her post only to feed the bonfire from time to time. As the day lightened, the battle noise grew louder, and Caroline saw a haze of gray smoke drifting into the western sky. There was no signal from Mama, though. Keeping her eye on Mama at the sail-loft window, Caroline paced anxiously back and forth.

A man on horseback galloped down the street toward the fighting, racing so fast that the animal's hooves sprayed mud behind them. Then several men in army uniform ran down the road in the opposite direction. Some carried guns. Some did not.

"Please—wait!" Caroline called after them. "What's happening?"

Two of the men kept running. The third paused. "God save us, girl, what are you doing here?"

Caroline quickly glanced up at Mama in the

window. No signal yet. "Tell me what's *happening*," she begged.

A few more men ran past the yard. The soldier ran a hand over his grimy face. "We're in retreat!"

Caroline grabbed his sleeve. "Where are the militiamen?"

"They're running too!"

An icy hand seemed to clutch Caroline's heart as she realized that the men running down the village's main street were fleeing from the British. "Is the battle lost, then?" she cried.

Instead of answering, the soldier pulled free and ran after his comrades.

In retreat. The words clanged in Caroline's mind like a bell. If the Americans were retreating, there might soon be no soldiers standing between the British and the shipyards. The signal to burn Abbott's could come any moment.

A stray cannonball shrieked overhead. Caroline dropped to a crouch, crooking her arms over her head for protection. *Crash!* She peeked up just in time to see the chimney on a nearby warehouse explode. Caroline screamed, but she hardly heard her own voice. The cannonball sent chimney bricks tumbling like a child's blocks.

"Caroline? *Caroline!*" It was her mother's voice, faint beneath the sounds of battle. Caroline raised her head and saw Mama standing at the open window with one hand pressed against her heart.

Caroline got gingerly to her feet. She was shaking, but she managed a little wave in her mother's direction. "I'm not hurt!" she yelled. From the window, Mama nodded.

The drifting smoke stung Caroline's eyes. Her ears ached from the deafening gunfire growing ever louder, ever closer. Beneath the roar, she heard shouts, a horse's wild whinny, crashes of timber and brick as another cannonball strayed into the village. More soldiers were running past the shipyard now, shouting and shoving, desperate to get away from the British.

"Stay steady," she ordered herself. She forced herself to stand and wait for the terrible order to burn the shipyard. It was the hardest thing she had ever done. Her knees trembled with longing to race after the fleeing soldiers. *I will not run,* Caroline told herself fiercely. *I will not abandon Mama. I will do whatever I must.* She repeated those words in her mind over and over.

Suddenly she heard Mama's voice again. Caroline looked up and saw Mama waving both arms frantically. "Go, Caroline!" Mama yelled. "It's time!"

Caroline ran and grabbed one of the torches. She needed both hands to control the heavy stick as she carefully tipped the end toward the bonfire. The oil-soaked cloth flared up at once.

With her heart thumping wildly, Caroline lifted the blazing stick and hurried to the skiff shed. She was clutching the torch so tightly that her fingers ached. Through the drifting smoke, she saw Mama run into the yard.

Caroline started to lower the torch toward the shavings and wood scraps she'd scattered against the shed walls the night before. Suddenly she thought of the joy in Papa's face when he'd returned to their shipyard after his long months away. Her arms froze, and tears brimmed in her eyes. *I can't do it!* she thought.

Then, in the midst of the noise and commotion, Caroline heard Mama's voice in her memory: *We must not let Abbott's fall into enemy hands!*

In her heart, Caroline knew that, hard as it was, she had to carry out the plan. Tears ran down her cheeks as she lowered the blazing torch to the wood scraps. "I'm sorry, Papa," she whispered.

The shavings caught quickly. Flames darted out in both directions, licking greedily at the wood. The fire raced around the shed, gaining height and speed. Soon the front wall was burning.

Caroline turned away. Through tears and smoke, she saw Mama splashing lamp oil against the gunboat's hull. Beyond her, across the harbor, black smoke billowed into the sky above Navy Point. The Americans had begun to burn their storehouses.

You must keep at it, Caroline told herself. She hurried to the nearest workshop. She dipped her torch, lighting wood shavings that she'd earlier piled against the wall.

"Wait!" someone bellowed.

Caroline looked up and saw Corporal Meyers running into the yard, waving his arms. "Stop!" he yelled. Chest heaving, he struggled to get the words out. "The storehouses—were set afire—by mistake!"

"But the Americans are retreating!" Caroline said. "I saw them running away."

Soon the front wall was burning. Caroline turned away. Through tears and smoke, she saw Mama splashing oil against the gunboat's hull.

"A few stood firm," Corporal Meyers told her. "And they saved the day."

Caroline's heart took a hopeful leap.

Corporal Meyers grinned. "Now it's the *British* who've turned tail! They're retreating back to Kingston!"

Caroline hurled her torch into the bonfire. She snatched her skirt high, away from the flames already beginning to flicker against the walls of the workshop. Then she grabbed a wooden bucket, dunked it into the nearby barrel, and poured water onto the flames. Corporal Meyers ran to help. With a few more bucketfuls, the fire was out and the shop was safe.

Gasping for breath, Caroline looked over the rest of the shipyard. The skiff shed's walls and roof were in flames, sending a plume of black smoke skyward. The shed stood apart from the other buildings, though. Caroline didn't think the fire would spread.

Mama stood like a statue by the gunboat, still holding her flaming torch. Caroline raced to join her. She could see the dark damp splotches on the gunboat where Mama had splashed the lamp oil.

"Heaven be praised," Mama whispered. "One

more moment, and I would have..." Her voice trailed away, as if she couldn't bear to put her thought into words.

Caroline pulled the torch from her mother's hands, ran across the yard, and threw it onto the bonfire. As she rejoined her mother, she spread her arms wide and twirled in a circle. "The shipyard is safe," she said joyfully. "Oh, Mama, our shipyard is safe!"

CHAPTER
FIVE
—
REUNION

A moment later, Corporal Meyers joined Caroline and Mama. "The battle is won," he declared, his eyes dark with emotion. "And the British did *not* get what they came for." He put a hand on the gunboat, and then he looked toward the navy shipyard, where the mighty frigate still stood proud and tall, almost ready to launch.

Relief made Caroline feel light inside. She reached up and patted the gunboat too.

"Ladies, I salute you," the corporal said. "And now, I must return to my post." With a nod, he hurried from the shipyard.

"Let's send a message home to Grandmother,"

Mama said, wiping her eyes with the back of one hand. "I suspect our work is not yet over. We must stay here until we are relieved."

It didn't take Caroline long to understand what Mama meant. Some of the American militiamen were in wild spirits as they celebrated their victory. Twice, Mama had to order several rowdy men away from the shipyard.

All morning Caroline stayed by the Abbott's sign at the street, searching for Papa's face among the crowds of returning men as they walked past. At midday, Mr. Tate and several of the workers straggled back to the yard. They were filthy, and one had a cut on his shoulder where a musket ball had grazed him—but all were accounted for.

"None of our men was seriously hurt," Mr. Tate reported. "I told those who have families to go home."

"Have you seen Papa?" Caroline asked anxiously.

Mr. Tate shook his head. "I'm sorry, we have not, Miss Caroline. I expect he'll be along soon."

The workers began cleaning up the yard. Mama joined Caroline by the Abbott's sign, watching. The afternoon inched by. The street was crowded with returning soldiers, and Caroline's eyes ached from searching for her father's face. *I didn't lose hope when Papa was a British prisoner,* she told herself. *I won't lose hope now.*

And then finally, *finally,* there he was. Caroline caught her breath when she spotted her father limping toward them. "Papa!" she shrieked.

Papa's face was grimy, and his eyes were bloodshot from smoke and exhaustion. But when he saw Caroline and Mama, he ran to them and swept them into a fierce hug.

Caroline clutched him so hard that her arms ached. She sent up a silent prayer of thanks for his safe return.

Then Mama led him gently to a nearby bench. The Abbotts settled together, Caroline snuggled close on one side of Papa and Mama on the other. "I've never been so glad to see you both," Papa said.

"We're fine," Caroline assured him.

"And we held the British off, by God," Papa murmured. "We held them off!"

Caroline pressed her cheek into his shoulder. Her heart was ready to burst.

After a moment, Papa asked, "What are you two doing here at the yard?"

Mama drew a deep breath. "Mr. Tate and the workers were called away to help fight the British," she told him. "Caroline and I couldn't leave the yard undefended."

Papa opened his mouth, then closed it again. Finally he said, "I can only imagine how difficult that must have been. I am proud of you both." After a moment he added quietly, "I heard that orders were given to burn the shipyards if need be." Papa looked slowly around the yard. Caroline wondered if he was imagining Abbott's in flames, just as she had.

Mama shuddered. "Fortunately, we heard the good news about the British retreat just in time. We had already lit our torches—"

"Oh, Papa, it was *awful!*" Caroline burst out. "I didn't think I could burn our yard. But I—I knew we couldn't let the British have it." She looked up at him. "Did we . . . do you think it would have been right to burn the yard?"

Papa wiped a hand over his face, which did nothing to improve his appearance. "You and Mama were faced with a dreadful situation, and you made the best decisions anyone could have." He squeezed their shoulders. "And in the end, nothing was lost."

That's not quite true, Caroline thought. She glanced toward all that was left of the skiff shed— ashes and blackened bits of wood. She knew she would never forget how it had felt to lower that torch and light the blaze. "One shed was lost," she said. "I set it on fire before we learned that the British were retreating. I'm sorry, Papa."

To her amazement, Papa laughed. "My dear daughter, the shed doesn't matter! My workers are safe. My business, and the gunboat, are safe. Best of all, my family is safe and together again."

Caroline nodded and let the last of her worries blow away like ash on the breeze.

Two weeks later, Caroline stood on the spot in Abbott's Shipyard where the skiff shed had once been. Grandmother had come to the yard, and so had the Hathaways and many of the Abbotts' friends and neighbors. The new gunboat was about to be launched!

It was a fine day for a celebration. Sunlight sparkled on Lake Ontario. A cool breeze kicked up little whitecaps on the water. The air smelled of tar and turpentine and the grease that workers were spreading on wooden tracks that would guide the boat into the lake. Caroline sniffed the air happily. Nothing, she thought, smelled quite so fine as a shipyard on the day of a boat launch!

Rhonda nudged Caroline with her elbow. "This is exciting!" she exclaimed. "I've never seen a gunboat launched before."

"Nor have I," Rhonda's father, Lieutenant Hathaway, chimed in. He had returned with most of the American expedition force the day after the Battle of Sackets Harbor. "Although I do know firsthand how valuable gunboats are. We can't win this war without them."

Caroline grinned. "Oh, look! The men are ready."

The shipyard workers took up places on both sides of the gunboat, which sat at the top of the tracks. Each man held a big mallet. Papa walked briskly among them, checking to make sure that all was in place. "Ready!" he yelled. "Now!"

70

The shipyard workers raised their mallets and struck at the wedges holding the ship steady. *Thump! Thump! Thump!* The wedges fell away. The gunboat began to slide down the greased wooden tracks. Caroline stood on tiptoe, holding her breath.

"There she goes!" Papa called. The gunboat splashed into the harbor, throwing up waves. Caroline laughed as she felt the spray on her face.

Rhonda jumped backward, clapping her hands. The workers whooped and hollered. The crowd cheered. Grandmother, who was seated nearby, gave Caroline a knowing nod. *You helped do this,* Grandmother's look said. *You helped defend this gunboat, which will now help defend us.*

Caroline's heart overflowed with pride. Soon the gunboat would be ready to strike at the British.

Mama tucked one hand through Papa's arm. Then she looked at Caroline and beckoned. Caroline joined her parents. "It's a fine gunboat," she told them.

"It is," Papa agreed. He smiled.

Caroline gazed out at the gunboat floating in the harbor, not far from the navy's enormous new frigate. *We showed the British that they don't control*

71

Caroline joined her parents. "It's a fine gunboat," she told them.
"It is," Papa agreed.

Lake Ontario, she thought, standing straight and tall. *And if they come back, we'll beat them again.*

She knew that the war would surely bring more hardships and difficult choices. Right this moment, though, Caroline felt ready to face whatever might come.

LOOKING BACK

AMERICA
IN
1812

Sackets Harbor today

Sackets Harbor, New York, is pretty and peaceful today. Tidy homes and summer cottages peek out from the tree-lined shore. Small sailboats bob on the gentle waves inside the harbor. In the breeze, the boats' ropes, or *rigging,* slap against the masts, making a musical *ping!* that sounds almost like chimes.

Visitors today might find it hard to believe that during Caroline's time, a fierce battle took place there. On

May 28, 1813, the British sent a fleet of warships across Lake Ontario to capture Sackets Harbor and destroy *General Pike,* a powerful

British warships attacking Sackets Harbor

new American warship being built there. The invaders knew that few American soldiers were on hand to defend the village. Like Rhonda Hathaway's father in the story, most soldiers and navy men were away on an expedition, hoping to capture British forts.

On that May day, though, the people of Sackets Harbor had luck—and nature—on their side. Before the British ships could reach the harbor, the wind died. The ships were stalled offshore, giving townspeople and farmers time to gather their muskets and prepare to fight.

The wind finally picked up at dawn on May 29, and the battle began. Just as the sun was rising, nearly 900 British soldiers landed on Horse Island, a small knob of land west of town.

Although Abbott's Shipyard and the events that take place there are fictional, the rest of the details described in Caroline's story are true. For hours that morning, cannons boomed and the sharp cracks of musket fire echoed through the air. The noise could be heard for miles. Many soldiers, both British and American, were killed.

The local men who served as part-time soldiers, or *militia*, had no experience in battle. They quickly became overwhelmed as they faced the better-trained,

A modern-day actor aims a musket as he helps re-enact the Battle of Sackets Harbor.

more powerful British forces. Many militiamen ran for their lives. Others, however, stood their ground and fought bravely, refusing to surrender.

When it seemed that the British were about to win, American soldiers set fire to their own storehouses on Navy Point—they did not want the enemy to capture their supplies. At just about the same time, though, the British gave up. The burning storehouses and their valuable supplies were lost, but the Americans had won the battle. Sackets Harbor was safe.

Soon after, shipbuilders finished work on *General Pike.* The grand warship patrolled the waters of Lake

The American frigate General Pike *is shown on the left. When it was built in Sackets Harbor in 1813, it was the largest warship ever to sail the Great Lakes.*

Ontario for the rest of the war. Although battles continued to be fought around the Great Lakes, Sackets Harbor was never attacked again.

Other cities weren't so lucky. On August 24, 1814, President James Madison got word that the British were planning to invade Washington, the nation's capital. Four thousand British soldiers were on their way to the city! The president made plans to join the American soldiers who were gathering to fight the British. He left the White House, where he and the First Lady, Dolley Madison, lived. He told Dolley to remain in the house until he came back.

First Lady Dolley Madison was famous for her beauty and hospitality—and for her bravery.

Dolley Madison was known as a fashionable woman and a fun-loving hostess who threw grand parties in the White House and served fancy foods like cake and pink ice cream to visitors. On that August afternoon, she showed that she was serious and brave as well. With enemy troops marching closer and closer, friends told Dolley she must flee. She refused to leave until she had gathered many important papers, along with a copy of a famous painting of the nation's first president, George Washington. When the British arrived that evening, they ate the supper that the Madisons had left behind. Then they set the White House ablaze, along with the Capitol and other government

buildings. Much of Washington was left in ashes. Thanks to Dolley Madison, though, important treasures had been saved.

The burning of Washington left Americans down-hearted and worried about whether the United States could win the war. They were given new hope a few weeks later, when the city of Baltimore, Maryland, was attacked. This time, things ended differently. Most of the citizens of Baltimore had pitched in to prepare. They built huge earth walls to protect U.S. soldiers. A com-mander hired Mary Pickersgill, a flagmaker and businesswoman, to make an American flag "so large that the British will have no dif-ficulty seeing it from a distance." Pickersgill worked for weeks, along with her 13-year-old daughter, her nieces, and an African American servant girl who worked for them, to stitch a flag 42 feet wide and 30 feet high.

Mary Pickersgill

The huge flag was hoisted above Fort McHenry, which guarded Baltimore Harbor. It warned the British that the soldiers there were brave and ready to fight.

The flag that Mary Pickersgill sewed is a national treasure. It is displayed at the Smithsonian's National Museum of American History in Washington, D.C.

This print shows "bombs bursting in air" over Fort McHenry during the battle that inspired "The Star-Spangled Banner," which is now America's national anthem.

On September 13, 1814, British warships began firing on Fort McHenry. Francis Scott Key, an American lawyer, watched from a ship outside the harbor. All night long, the battle raged. Rockets flew, flaming and red, into the fort. Bombs burst overhead, filling the sky with a thick haze of smoke. Key was anxious. In the dark, he couldn't tell whether British soldiers had managed to get inside the fort. But as the sun rose and the haze cleared the next morning, he caught sight of the huge American flag. It was still flying high atop the fort's walls. The Americans had kept the harbor safe!

Key was overjoyed. That morning, he began writing a poem about the battle to honor the soldiers who had defended the fort. "O say can you see, by the

Francis Scott Key

81

dawn's early light..." he wrote. He set the words to a familiar tune, and "The Star-Spangled Banner" quickly became popular across the country. As years passed, people began singing it on the Fourth of July and even at sports events.

In 1931, Congress passed a law declaring the song our national anthem. Some citizens were against the song. They wanted a peaceful anthem, not one about war. But "The Star-Spangled Banner" had touched many people's hearts. Today, when Americans sing "The Star-Spangled Banner," the words are reminders of the heroic men and women who have defended our country during wartime. The last few words—"the land of the free and the home of the brave"—may also make us think about what freedom means to us, and about the ways that even ordinary people can be brave.

A SNEAK PEEK AT

CHANGES FOR

Caroline

Caroline leaves Sackets Harbor to help Uncle Aaron and
cousin Lydia on their new farm. She expects to work
hard—but she doesn't *expect to face a thief!*

"It's so nice to have you here," Lydia told Caroline as they walked to the cowshed the next morning. "I've been lonely since we left Sackets Harbor. I—" She stopped suddenly and stared toward the shed.

Caroline felt a flicker of alarm. "What's wrong?"

Lydia pointed to the door, which hung slightly open. "I'm sure I latched it last night."

"The cows!" Caroline cried. She flung the shed door open and ran inside, with Lydia right on her heels. She felt limp with relief when she saw Garnet and Minerva.

Lydia sagged against the wall. "Oh, thank heavens. Maybe I only *thought* I'd latched the door."

Or maybe, Caroline thought, *a thief has his eye on Garnet and Minerva.*

"I'll tell Papa later," Lydia said. "For now, let's see how our girls are doing this morning."

Caroline and Lydia leaned on the stall railing, watching Garnet nurse hungrily from her mother. Minerva seemed impatient. Every few minutes she'd walk restlessly away from Garnet.

"See that?" Lydia asked. "Minerva wants Garnet to start feeding on her own."

"What will Garnet eat now?" Caroline asked.

"This morning she'll start by learning to drink milk from a bucket," Lydia said. "Then we'll gradually change that to water. She'll learn to eat hay and grass and vegetables, too." She grasped the rope halter fastened around Minerva's head. "I'm going to take Minerva outside so that Garnet can't nurse. You stand by the door and close it before Garnet can follow us."

Caroline hesitated. "What if Minerva pokes you with her horns?"

"Minerva is as gentle as a lamb," Lydia assured her. "Little Garnet is the one you have to watch out for!"

Lydia led Minerva out to a small pen behind the shed. When Caroline shut the door, Garnet bawled in protest.

Caroline gently patted Garnet. She liked how the calf's thick hair felt both soft and bristly. "Poor thing," Caroline told her. "I know just how you feel. I miss my mother, too."

Garnet turned her head. She seemed to be listening carefully.

"And silly Lydia told me I had to watch out for you," Caroline scoffed. By the time Lydia returned

85

with a bucket of milk, Caroline and Garnet were getting along just fine.

"Time for Garnet's first lesson," Lydia said.

"May I try?" Caroline asked eagerly.

Lydia handed her the bucket. "Dip your fingers in the milk," she instructed.

Caroline put her fingers into the warm milk. "Now what?"

"Put your hand in front of Garnet's mouth and let her suck from your fingers," Lydia said. "Calves don't have upper teeth, so she can't hurt you."

"Want some milk?" Caroline asked, stretching her hand toward Garnet. She held her breath. The calf sniffed once before taking Caroline's fingers into her mouth. Garnet's tongue felt rough, and she sucked with so much force that for a moment Caroline wasn't sure she'd be able to get her fingers back! Once the milk was gone, however, she was able to pull her hand away.

Garnet sucked milk from Caroline's fingers several times. Each time, Caroline held her hand closer and closer to the bucket.

"Now," Lydia said finally, "keep your fingers right at the surface of the milk."

Caroline dipped her fingers back into the milk. Garnet looked at her hand and snorted.

"Come now, Garnet," Caroline coaxed. "You can do it."

Instead of putting her nose into the milk, Garnet butted her head against the pail—*hard*. Thrown off balance, Caroline stumbled and couldn't stay on her feet. She landed on her backside. A spray of milk landed on her.

Lydia sputtered with laughter. "I told you she was strong!"

Once she was over her surprise, Caroline laughed too. She rose to her feet and dusted herself off. Bits of straw clung to the back of her skirt, and milk and cow drool streaked the front. "I thought Garnet was ready to drink from the pail! Why did she hit it?"

"She wasn't being mean," Lydia said. "She butts her head against Minerva when she wants milk. It's her way of saying she's hungry."

The calf gazed up at Caroline with her big, dark eyes as if to say, *I'm sorry you fell down.*

"You're a rascal," Caroline scolded her lightly. "Next time you want something, be more polite!"

Once the girls had finished tending the cows and

*Garnet butted her head against the pail, **hard**. Caroline landed on her backside. A spray of milk landed on her. Lydia sputtered with laughter.*

cleaning their stall, they tackled
the huge vegetable garden. In the
nearest row, small, lacy carrot plants
had poked through the soil in a tidy line, but tall
weeds were choking them. Caroline knelt and began
pulling the weeds carefully. As she worked, she
wondered if Grandmother was weeding the garden
at home. Was she managing?

I'm needed here, Caroline reminded herself. Soon
the wave of homesickness passed, and Caroline
finished weeding her row. "This looks much better,"
she said, sitting back on her heels.

Lydia wiped sweat from her cheek, leaving a
smudge of dirt behind. "Papa will want his midday
meal soon," she said. She pointed to a far corner of
the garden. "There's some asparagus back there that
might be ready to eat. Would you look?"

Caroline made her way to the asparagus patch.
The garden's far corner was thick with tall weeds.
Caroline pushed them aside, searching. Where was
the asparagus? She didn't see any of the
straight green spears poking from the
earth. She knelt and crawled back and
forth, parting weeds with her hands.

Then she stopped short. "Oh no," she moaned. No wonder she'd had trouble finding the asparagus! Every stalk had been sliced off, leaving just the barest nub of green above the soil. "Lydia? Come look at this."

Lydia joined her and stared at the asparagus nubs. "Someone *cut* those."

"I'm afraid so," Caroline said. "And stole every last stalk."

Lydia stamped one foot. "First a pan of milk went missing, and now this. I was counting on that asparagus!" She glared at the damage for a moment. Then she sighed. "I'd better fetch Papa. He'll want to see this."

When Uncle Aaron saw the nubs, he muttered something under his breath. Then he rubbed his face with one hand. "We can't have any more thievery on our place," he said. "If the scoundrel stole vegetables, he might steal Minerva or Garnet next."

Caroline felt a hitch in her chest. Lydia and her father needed those cows. Besides . . . the thought of a thief leading those sweet animals away was unbearable.

MEET CAROLINE
When the British attack Caroline's village, she
makes a daring choice that helps to win the day.

CAROLINE'S SECRET MESSAGE
Caroline and Mama take a *dangerous journey*
to the British fort where Papa is held prisoner.

A SURPRISE FOR CAROLINE
Caroline finds herself on thin ice after
friendship troubles lead to a bad decision.

CAROLINE TAKES A CHANCE
When a warship threatens American supplies,
can Caroline's little fishing boat turn it away?

CAROLINE'S BATTLE
As a battle rages right in her own village,
Caroline faces a terrible choice.

CHANGES FOR CAROLINE
Caroline pitches in on her cousin's new farm—
and comes home to a wonderful surprise.

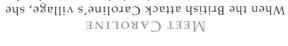